GPEP
1/21

GPEP

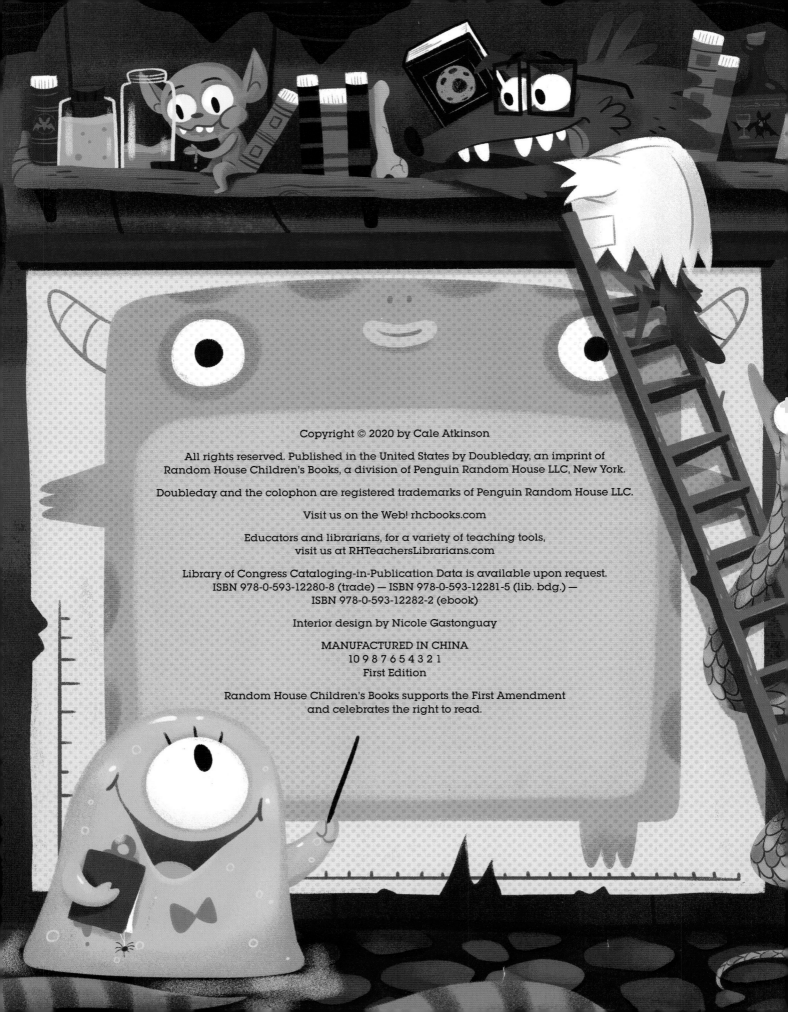

Visit us on the Web! rhcbooks.com

Educators and librarians, for a variety of teaching tools,
visit us at RHTeachersLibrarians.com

Library of Congress Cataloging-in-Publication Data is available upon request.
ISBN 978-0-593-12280-8 (trade) — ISBN 978-0-593-12281-5 (lib. bdg.) —
ISBN 978-0-593-12282-2 (ebook)

Interior design by Nicole Gastonguay

MANUFACTURED IN CHINA
10 9 8 7 6 5 4 3 2 1
First Edition

MONSTERS

You've heard the spooky stories, the rumors, the whispers.
It's time we shone a light on what *really* hides in the shadows.

Say hello to the masters of Monstronomy.

PROFESSOR BATULA McFANG

Bats and Blood Specialist

PROFESSOR BLOBBINS

Goop Whiz

PROFESSOR HOWLSWORTH

Moon Chaser

TINA THE ZOMBIE

Expert on Brraaaiiinnnnns

These creatures of the night aren't here to frighten. They are here to enlighten! Will you be eaten along the way? Well, there's always a chance, so keep your wits about you and hold on to your juicy brain.

So just what makes a monster a monster? Is it a diabolical laugh? A terrible smell? Or the fact that some of their teeth are longer than your legs? Let's find out!

OFFICIAL MONSTER CHECKLIST

EYES:

- [ ] One bloodshot
- [ ] Glowing
- [ ] Seven stink eyes
- [ ] Flaming pupils

BODY:

- [ ] Purple fur
- [ ] Fireproof scales
- [ ] Sticky slime
- [ ] Poison prickles

TEETH:

- [ ] Yellow fangs
- [ ] Gruesome tusks
- [ ] Pointy chompers
- [ ] Chunky chompers

FEATURES:

- [ ] Bony wings
- [ ] Gnarly claws
- [ ] Curly tentacles
- [ ] Jagged horns

CLOTHING:

- [ ] Spooky cape
- [ ] Old-timey duds
- [ ] Mud and leaves
- [ ] Ripped bandages

ODORS:

- [ ] Limburger cheese
- [ ] Raunchy toe jam
- [ ] Garbage juice
- [ ] Rancid leftovers

Is that a monster hiding under your bed?!
Use the checklist to be sure!

MONSTER FACT

Frankenstein is the name of the scientist who made the monster. The actual monster has no name!

Ahhh! I have no name!

What would *you* name him?

2: Biology

Now that you know *what* a monster is, it's time to dig deeper into what's going on beyond the fur and fangs.

Common name:	Monster
Scientific name:	*Super scarius*
Family:	Toothica Sharpidae
Territory:	Closets, crypts, dungeons, and under beds
Communication:	Grunts, howls, murmurs, and sneezes
Defense:	Teeth, claws, and slime
Name for young:	Furbs
Life span:	Forever, plus 4–5 years
Behavior:	Friendly, unless cranky

Unlike humans, monsters aren't limited to one brain, heart, and stomach.

3: Monster Types

Monsters come in all shapes and sizes.

Vampire

Common, everyday monsters include:

Cyclops

Ogre

Troll

Hydra

Sea Monster

Yeti

Swamp Thing

Chupacabra

Blob

Ghost

Mummy

Werewolf

Zombie

Bigfoot

Goblin

Wert

Lesser-known and rare monsters include:

Yern Yern

Frumple

Snurt

Blunderblort

Kurplat

Skeepie

Durgle

Splonk

Gromp

Zoof

Sloof

Catapus

Richard

Taffadills

While monsters love to have a good time, not every day can be a wild rumpus. Monsters have to take care of themselves, and it's not always easy!

With all those teeth, many monsters find themselves back in the dentist's chair again and again.

While some monsters spend their time butt naked, other monsters go through clothing at a fast rate.

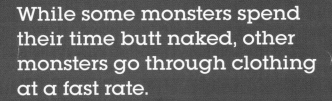

Whether it's overgrown fur or out-of-control claws, some monsters need constant grooming to look their most horrifying!

Riding the bus or shopping at the market can be tricky when you're a monster. Good thing there's . . .

Sal's Bargain-Price Human Disguises!

Your one-stop shop for all things human!

MONSTER DEALS!

Every monster's #1 choice when needing to be out among humans.

- Costumes
- Masks
- Odors
- Legs
- Hats

SCENT OF A HUMAN

- Rated 4.5 on MonsterAdvisor
- Satisfaction scare-anteed

FREE HUMAN MASK with this coupon!*

*Must be a monster to redeem. Only valid at Haunted Hills location.

Self-care is important to keep a monster from becoming a grumpy, grumbling menace.

Like humans, monsters need to have fun and let off some steam.

Favorite monster activities include:

Competitive game nights

Arm wrestling

Scare-offs

Stand-up comedy

Cooking

Scare-aoke

It's no secret that monsters love to eat!
Each monster has its own tastes,
and these can differ widely.

Truly the best dish for any monster is blood-boiled lobster with blood butter and a finely aged bottle of blood.

That is super gross. What monsters really enjoy is a nice bone with a side of kibble.

Sounds more like dog food. Monsters prefer a mouthwatering buffet of garbage.

Brains!

BRAINS!

BRRAAAIIINNNNNS!

6: Habitats and Homes

Monsters love having somewhere to put up their feet or tentacles after a long day of monstering around.

Let's ring the doorbell at Tina's digs, a cozy yet tastefully decorated grave.

BRAIN FOOD

Common items
found in a
zombie's home:
* Cooking cauldron
* Spider garden
* Personal slime tub
* Pet alligator
* Cozy coffin bed

7: Monster History

Throughout the ages, monsters have played a role in history, from prehistoric times to the present day.

Down in the Unnatural History Cryptorium, we find the Hall of Famous Monsters.

DR. UNDEROOS:
First monster to
wear underpants

SMOOCHY THE TERRIBLE:
World's cutest monster

HOOVES HAMINGTON:
First were-pig

IRIS THE SECOND:
First cyclops
with two eyes

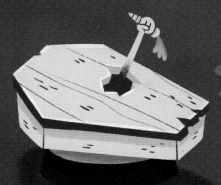

TOFU CAULIFLOWER:
First vegetarian
zombie

SPIKE THE FRIENDLY:
First monster to be
friends with a human

INVISI-BILL:
World's smallest
monster

BLECHULA:
First blood-intolerant
vampire

8: Fears

It's hard to imagine a monster having anything to be scared of, but monsters can have all types of fears. Don't even get me started on garlic!

Mummies are terrified of playful puppies.

Sea monsters have a phobia of sand getting between their toes.

Gromps have a deep fear of beards.

Werewolves freak out when they hear a vacuum.

If there is one thing that spooks all monsters
more than anything else, it's

HUMANS.

They are unpredictable and sneaky and seem to
always have it out for monsters.

It only takes one human to yell "MONSTER!"
And before you can say "Dracula's underpants,"
there's a full-on human freak-out.

Monsters are very wary of getting too close to a
human, as they never know how humans will react.

9: Monster-Human Interactions

It's not uncommon to find out you're roommates with a ghost, goblin, or gremlin, down in the basement or stuffed in your closet.

It's a basic fact that one in every three homes has a monster hiding under a bed. What are they doing under there? Take a look for yourself!

Am I going to be eaten?

While monsters may send a chill down your spine, the truth is most of them are completely harmless. In fact, many monsters are working hard to change humans' negative view of them.

Like anyone, though, monsters can have an off day or be in a bad mood, and that may include swallowing a mailman or eating a car.

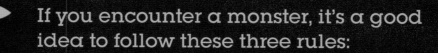

If you encounter a monster, it's a good idea to follow these three rules:

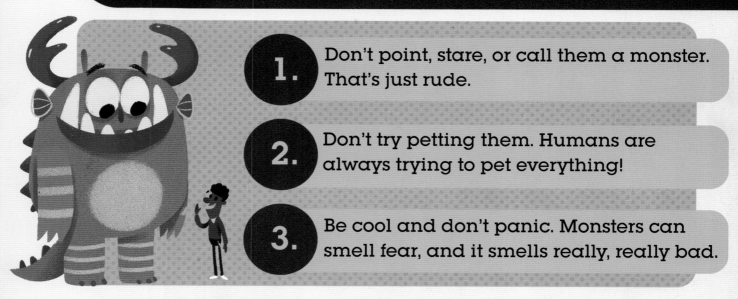

1. Don't point, stare, or call them a monster. That's just rude.

2. Don't try petting them. Humans are always trying to pet everything!

3. Be cool and don't panic. Monsters can smell fear, and it smells really, really bad.

Keeping those things in mind, it should be easy to become BFFs with any monster you meet!

You've made it to the end without losing any brains or body parts! You have earned the right to be an honorary Monster Scientist.

Next time you hear a bump in the night, think back to all you have learned here, and remember: It's probably more scared of you than you are of it.

The only thing left to do is howl in celebration!

Monstronomy
Diploma

successfully finished this course
and earned the haunted title of

Monster Scientist

It is your duty to study, protect, and care for
all the monsters of the world.

McFang

Professor Batula McFang

HOWLSWORTH

Professor Howlsworth

BLObbin$

Professor Blobbins

BRaiinnns!

Tina